Zeke and Lily

Once Upon a Beginning

By

Zorro Daddy

Zorro Daddy Publications

Before you get started …

Role playing, in a real life sense or online, is *assuming identities which are different from those in our everyday lives.* Countless themes in role playing cater to sexual preference, power exchange, fantasy and many more. Some affect the individuals in a physical manner. Others affect their emotions. Some even go so deeply as to affect the heart, the mind and the soul completely. One such role playing theme is **infantilism**.

This book is by a heterosexual male. So the roles of infantilism used in this story are from a straight point of view.

What I write is always journey and an exploration into the subject of infantilism. It is not a book that gives in-depth explanation of infantilism, just a brief overview here in the introduction. This is simply a collection of my literature about the subject, and Every word you read is a piece of my heart.

So, what is Infantilism? The only definitions you will read in this book are here. Firstly:

Infantilism – retention of childish physical, mental or emotional qualities in adult life.

Infantilism is a form of age play where someone regresses into the behavior and personality of a baby or toddler. They choose to do this for a number of reasons, ranging from a need for release of tension to the desire to live without adult responsibility.

Whether infantilism is something that is shocking to you or not, you absolutely must understand one thing right away.

ABDL-minded people become enraged when a parallel is drawn between infantilism and pedophilia. Infantilism is role playing between consenting adults. Pedophilia is a hideous crime that involves minors. There is no parallel between the two. It is the theme of the role playing in infantilism that leads people to call it pedophilia. This theme includes a care giver and a care receiver. An adult who role plays as a parent, and an adult who role plays as a baby, but they are both adults.

In the writings of this book, those two roles are "Daddy" and "BabyGirl". There is a dominant figure and a submissive one, much like in BDSM (Bondage, Discipline, Sado-Masochism) roles. Infantilism eliminates the BDSM part of it.

Some adults have sexual interest in infantilism. Others have no sexual interest in it. This varies by the individual. Some choose to live infantilism as their lifestyle while others choose to role play it on occasion.

That being said, there are a few terms I would like to explain before you get started.

AB (Adult Baby): An adult that chooses to regress to a state of mind she had when she was an infant. She will often retain the personality, and mannerisms of an infant. She finds interest in infantile things like toys, pacifiers, bottles, baby clothing, etc. Some even return to wearing a diaper. She submits to being treated, regarded, spoken to, and cared for as if she were a baby. She assumes the role of a baby/toddler.

DL (Diaper Lover): An adult who wears a diaper, but has no role playing as an AB.

BabyGirl: An adult female. Just as in everyday life, this is a term of endearment for a girl, but within the role playing of infantilism, it means so much more. Explained as you read through this book, but please understand she is an adult.

If you aren't aware of what infantilism is, hopefully this book will give you incite.

Once Upon a Beginning

Every story has a beginning. Before Zeke and Lily got to know one another and before they took a Caribbean cruise to the Bahamas they were perfect strangers who shared a common interest in a fetish. This is the story of the day they first met face-to-face at a mall in Lancaster County, PA. It is the prequel to the story: "Zeke and Lily - Overnight" which is followed by the short novel: "Zeke and Lily - Making a Memory."

Once Upon A Beginning...

Lily Paddington got into her car and flipped the sun visor down, using the mirror to check her make-up and hair. A trip to the mall usually meant she was about to go on one of her relentless shopping sprees. But not today and not on this trip. This was a very important day, and one that she didn't want to be late for. But she was all ready late and it only made her more nervous than she all ready was.

All the phone calls and emails led to this. She was actually going to meet him face-to-face. Can fairy tales really come true? This was the question on her mind as she pulled out of her driveway on Lime Street and drove past the General Hospital in the center of Lancaster City. Her destination: Park City Mall. At that very moment, there was a guy waiting for her in the J. C. Penney's food court whom she had met online. She was going there to meet the guy who might be able to show her that fairy tales can come true.

She turned onto Lemon Street and then onto Harrisburg Pike. She was practically begging for a speeding ticket. Passing through Franklin and Marshall College, she began to wonder what he would be like in person.

His profile and emails told a story to her. The chat she had with him online showed that he wasn't obsessed about ABDL and had an engaging life beyond it. On the phone, his voice had a calming tone to it. They never ran out of things to talk about. But now, she was going to met him in person.

She recalled talking with him about what a person's eyes can say about them without ever saying a word. She wondered what his eyes would say about him, and if her eyes would make it obvious that she was nervous.

That nervousness as well as the excitement she was feeling had given her a stirred up feeling in her tummy, like butterflies were fluttering around inside her. With every thought, she got herself more and more worked up.

She reached under her dress and felt the elastic edging of the diaper she was wearing. She smiled, happy that she had convinced herself to wear it and it only added to the anticipation she felt for an evening she hoped she would never forget. But her mind still worried. Maybe she shouldn't have worn the diaper, but she wanted to see what she would feel like if she were wearing it when she met him. It would be a heart-pounding experience for sure.

She pulled into the Penney's/Sears parking lot at breakneck speed, finding the closest spot to the entrance. She parked and flipped the visor down again, taking a final look at her make-up and hair.

She got out of the car and began briskly walking to the entrance, but then slowed her pace down when she realized how noisy her diaper was. She began to worry that she might be "discovered". Wearing a diaper in public was something she had only ever tried once before. She remembered it was a thrill to be out in public in a diaper, but she couldn't bring herself to get out of her car when she did it before. So she found herself in uncharted territory as she walked to the entrance.

She walked a little more slowly up to the covered entrance area. Walking towards the glass doors, she could see people inside. Her hands began shaking as she reached for the door handle and opened the door. As she walked in, she lowered her chin and began to scan the crowd of people in front of her, looking for him.

There were lines of people standing at the food counters. Every seat at every table in the eating area was filled. Little kids ran by. People walked in and out of the Penney's entrance straight ahead. People were riding the escalators up and down to the main floor. There was no way she would be able to find him in this sea of bodies. Then she got an idea.

She took out her phone and speed dialed his number, listening for his ringtone. He said his ringtone for her was "Be my Baby" by the Ronettes. She listened as best she could through the noise in the room. Then behind her at one of the tables she heard a cell phone ring.

"The night we met I knew I needed you so," she heard coming from a phone. "And if I had the chance I'd never let you go."

The guy sitting at the table stood up as the ringtone continued to its end.

"So won't you say you love me? I'll make you so proud of me," she heard as she slowly crossed over to him, taking one last chance to straighten the yellow summer dress she was wearing. "We'll make 'em turn their heads every place we go."

Lily folded her hands in front of her, clutching her jean jacket. Suddenly, everything around her seemed to fade away and get quiet. He stood almost six feet tall. She had to look up to see his face. This didn't shock her. She knew how tall he was. As he turned around, she saw the Kansas City Chiefs hat she forgot she was supposed to be looking for.

Then their eyes met.

"Zeke?" she asked softly.

"Lily," he said, smiling.

She was as nervous as could be, but still batted her eyelashes and smiled as she gracefully walked over to him and embraced him. She was still trembling from having been late, but his arms wrapped around her and she experienced a feeling she had never felt before … little. She stopped trembling instantly and placed her head on his chest, listening to his heart beat while feeling the warmth from his body.

They ended the embrace and she took a moment to look into his eyes before speaking. This gave her that moment to see what his eyes said to her, as well as another second to figure out what the first thing she said to him would be.

She could see tenderness and kindness in his eyes, in the way he smiled, and how he spoke to her. All initial indications made her believe he was a good guy, but he would have to show his heart to her before she would trust him further. Still, her cautiousness didn't inhibit her happiness.

"Sorry I'm late. I have butterflies and I'm a little nervous," she rambled to him. "Traffic was moving so slow, and … well, how was that for a hello? Pretty strange, huh? Yeah, I know. I'm a little quirky."

"You look beautiful," he said, as her nervousness began settling. "And you just took my breath away."

His words stopped her in her tracks. She was expecting him to say something sweet and probably forgetful, not memorable.

"So you are the guy on the other end of the phone," she said while recovering from the compliment.

"And you are the girl who came out of nowhere," he said while offering his right hand to her. "I'll never forget that first message."

She took his right hand with her left hand and they began walking towards the escalators.

"I'll never forget your response," she said, smiling while nibbling her bottom lip. "Do you remember the first question you asked me?"

"Yeah. I asked you if you were really female," he said, laughing.

"Okay. That's right," she said, returning the laugh. "How about the second question you asked me?"

"I believe I asked you what you dreamed about when you went to bed at night," he said.

"And do you remember my response?" she asked with a playful twinkle in her eyes.

"Yes, you said it was hard to put into words," he replied as they stepped off the escalator and headed down the mall. "Come to think of it…that's all you said. You never answered the question."

"I will," she said sweetly as they stepped onto the escalator.

"Okay," he replied with a laugh. "Let me know when some time."

"Patience," she said with a smile. "That's not information I want to tell you in the middle of a mall."

"Speaking of which … why did you choose Park City Mall to be our meeting place?" he asked. "It's shaped like a spider. Aren't you afraid of spiders?"

"I'm afraid of every little creepy crawly that exists," she answered.

"So I suppose that a camping trip in the future is out of the question?" he asked with a grin.

"Way, way, way out of the question," she said, laughing. "I picked this mall because my grandfather used to bring me here when I was a little girl. He would buy me whatever birthday present I wanted and then he'd take me to McDonald's, which used to be right there."

Lily pointed to the store right next to the escalator.

"But now it's a music store," she said. "I would always get something at KayBee Toy & Hobby."

"Which is now a dollar store," Zeke said. "It's sad how things change like that."

Zeke was a very normal sounding guy. He was easy to talk to and she didn't have the impulse to run away when she met him. This was a good thing. They made their way through the mall, headed towards Damon's Barr and Grille. She began to feel more comfortable with him. But it wasn't hard to find that comfort. She knew a lot about him all ready, but in person she was re-discovering the comfort she felt when just talking to him on the phone.

"What kind of toys did you play with when you were young?" she asked.

"I was a Lego Maniac," Zeke replied. "And He-Man. I take it you were a Barbie Doll girl?"

"Of course," she said, developing a playful glow in her eyes. "And I still am."

"I bet you are," Zeke said with a smile as they approached the entrance for Damon's Bar and Grille.

"It's almost like a hobby," she said as he opened the restaurant door for her.

"A hobby, huh?" he asked.

"It's a little more than a hobby…much like other things," she surreptitiously whispered in his ear as she walked in.

They were taken to their table with very little wait. The dinner rush had come and gone. So the restaurant wasn't crowded, and they could talk a little more easily about "other" topics. But not just yet.

"So what is the one hobby you cherish more than any other?" Zeke asked as he pushed her chair in.

"I like to lie in bed at night and gaze up at the stars in the sky through my window," she said. "I read that your dreams often tell you things about yourself that you never knew. Do you dream?"

"Yes, but I never remember my dreams when I wake up," he said.

"Why not?" she asked.

"I wish I knew," he replied.

"What do think they might say about you if you could remember them?" she asked.

"They'd probably tell me to stop dreaming and get some sleep. I have a bit of a sleeping problem," he said, smiling.

“What do your dreams say about you?”

“Okay, okay. I’ll tell you,” she said, laughing. “My dreams tell me about a love for infantilism I never knew I had.”

“Oh wow. Tell me about the first ABDL dream you had,” he said.

The waiter arrived with their appetizer, and they paused from their conversation until he left.

“Okay,” she began, preparing herself to reveal this dream to someone for the first time. “I woke up in a crib wearing the cutest little pink footed pajamas I had ever seen. It felt so warm. I was lying on my tummy and I turned over and sat up. My hair was super curly and I had pigtails. The crib was filled with all kinds of stuffed animals…zebras, giraffes, elephants, teddy bears, monkeys, puppies and kittens.”

“But no lions or tigers, I suppose,” he said.

“No, and I didn’t see Toto the dog either,” she laughed. “I looked up and saw a mobile above me with small ducks and chicks and goats and sheep dangling down from it on different colored pieces of ribbon,” she said, taking a sip of her soda. “I lied back down, rubbed my eyes with my hands and then I looked at my fingers. They were so tiny.”

She paused to take a drink, and then continued on.

"Then my tummy began to rumble, and I felt a hunger like never before. Almost like fate had decreed it to happen, the door to the room opened," she said, taking a bite of the appetizer. "Someone walked in. The light was dim in the room, but I could tell it was a guy. He was too far away for me to make out his face. He was very blurry. I squinted my eyes, but even as he got closer to me, he still remained blurry."

"Who did you think he was?" Zeke asked.

"I have no idea, but for some reason I didn't fear him. I was actually overjoyed to see him," she recalled. "He lowered the side of the crib and placed a baby bottle between my lips. I kept trying to make out his face as I started drinking from the bottle. It was filled with a sweet-tasting liquid that I savored on my tongue as I swallowed it. I clutched the bottle with both hands and nursed it down."

Lily paused from telling the story and shifted in her seat, re-adjusting her diaper but doing so as to not alert Zeke she was wearing it.

"Then what happened?" Zeke asked.

"This next part is really embarrassing. I don't know if I can tell it," she said as her shoulders shrunk up and her chin lowered slightly.

"It's okay Lily," he said as he touched her hand, used his finger to raise her chin, and made eye contact. "This dream was very important. It had a lasting effect on you, and found a way to touch your heart. Please go on."

The waiter appeared with their meals and then left. Lily hesitantly continued the story.

"He was rubbing my tummy as I drank from the bottle," she said in a whispered voice. "He unbuttoned the lower half of my pajamas and pulled my legs out. His hands felt so kind and his touch was so gentle. I felt his hand slide under me as he felt the back of my diaper. I didn't even know I was wearing a diaper. He unfastened the diaper, folded it down from the front. Then his left hand grabbed my ankles, put them together, and lifted my legs into the air. He was so very careful with how he touched me. He was very loving and nice."

"It sounds like it came to him naturally," Zeke said.

"Yeah, and he was so much bigger than me. I felt so little and helpless in his grasp. But I was never scared by him. And …" she said, pausing as she buried her hands in her face as she tried to conquer her embarrassment.

"It's okay," Zeke whispered back softly.

She lowered her hands and continued.

"I had pooped in my diaper, and he began to wipe my bottom clean. I was an awkward feeling, but one that I welcomed. While still holding my legs and bottom in the air, he unfolded a new diaper and placed it underneath me. As he did this, I began to feel like a baby. Here was this guy who was so very endearing and nice to me. And he was caring for me as if I were a baby. It was such a wonderful feeling."

"You bonded emotions with him," Zeke said.

"Yeah and I felt a love for him that was different than any other love I had ever felt for anyone," she continued. "He lowered my legs back down and then powdered me. He fastened my diaper into place. Right at that moment, I finished my bottle. He placed the bottle on the crib mattress and unbuttoned the top of my pajamas. He lifted me out of the pajamas and up into his arms. I rested my head on his shoulders and closed my eyes. His body was so warm and it felt so good to be next to him."

"He sounds like he was a very attentive Daddy," Zeke said.

"He was," Lily confirmed. "I looked up at his face for a moment, but it was still blurry. He kissed my forehead and I returned to resting on his shoulder. He began walking around the room with me in his arms. He bounced me up and down very, very slowly while he patted my bottom and my back. This must have gone on for a few minutes before I finally burped. Then, I became very sleepy. He placed a pacifier in my mouth, and in a matter of a few seconds, I was asleep. And that was the end of my dream."

"Everybody has a different starting point when they fell in love with infantilism. That is the most incredible, touching story I think I've ever heard," Zeke said with awe in his voice.

"I woke up and had such a collection of butterflies in my tummy, I curled up in a ball and rolled around," she said, smiling. "And those butterflies return to my tummy every time I get nervous or when thoughts of being a baby enter my mind."

"Do you have a lot of dreams like that?" Zeke asked.

"Some are a little different, but in every dream, I get to be a little girl again," she said. "I get to return to that time in every girl's life when everybody loved her, unconditionally. When she was held and hugged and kissed. Everybody made a fuss over her, and played with her and made her laugh. She could run around and bounce up-n-down and do whatever made her happy. Nobody wanted anything from her, except a smile and to hear her say she loved them."

"You probably never feel that way as an adult female," Zeke said.

"Never, but I don't feel like an adult inside, and as a BabyGirl I don't have to act like one," she said.

"How does it make you feel?" he asked.

"You feel safety, security, comfort, and you learn how to trust people with your heart. When you're bathed and fed and spoken to like a baby, and when someone treats you like a baby, you begin to feel like a baby," she said, smiling. "It feels wonderful. Your tummy gets a flustered feeling inside. Your skin tingles and you just wanna curl up in a ball and giggle. When you're not in charge of your life, your senses hunger for someone to take control of you. When you know everything will be taken care of, then you stop worrying and start enjoying yourself.... But that's a really dangerous wish to have in my heart."

"Why?" he asked.

"Without the right person who sees it the same way, I'll not only be disappointed, but I'll be putting myself in a dangerous situation," she answered.

"But what if the situation were right, like in your dreams?" he asked.

"Then I'd be in Heaven. I'd be the luckiest girl in the world. A helpless feeling of being little would come over me, and I'd imagine I would find a new sense of love," she said with a twinkle in her eyes.

"A new sense of love? What would that be?" he asked, inquisitively.

“I have no idea. I have never felt that little before but I anxiously want to know what it feels like,” she admitted.

“Babies have a different wardrobe, toys, accessories, you name it. If you could have any baby item, what would it be? Better yet, dream really big. Name them all.”

“Bright colored pacifiers and stuffed animals galore. Nighties and onesies and Baby Ts and more,” she said, starting to laugh at how she rhymed.

“This is beginning to sound like a song from a musical,” Zeke said with a smile. “How about bath times with bubbles and stories read from rocking chairs? Spaghetti meals and finger food and ribboned pigtails in your hair?”

Lily laughed out loud and then covered her mouth.

“That all sounds wonderful,” she said, enjoying his entertainment. “Keep going. I’ll tell you when you get one wrong.”

“Baby Bottles for nursing and blankets for wrapping. Barbies to play with and cribs for your napping,” he said. “Night lights to brighten your world as you dream. Mountains of pillows to jump on with glee,” he said.

Lily clapped her hands with excitement, and then got quiet remembering where they were.

“One more,” she said while resting her chin on your hands, taken in by how creative he was.

“Footed pajamas that snuggle you sweetly. Diapers that cover your bottom discreetly,” he said as they finished their meals. “Nursery time nighty-nights, soft lullabies. Endless your smile and twinkling eyes.”

“I think you named it all,” she said with a wide smile.

They left Damon’s Grille and entered the mall. It was Lily’s plan to not enter the mall after they ate if she felt uncomfortable. She would say goodbye and polite leave. She had it all worked out in her mind. But she never felt uncomfortable and the butterflies of “nervousness” that plagued her stomach on the way to the mall were gone. They were replaced by butterflies of “elation” that were telling her she was at the beginning of something wonderful.

She had a back-up plan ready to go if her escape plan was needed, but she wasn’t able to get away from him. Her back-up plan was to go to the Bath & Body Works store for what she would call “a necessary purchase”. She would walk into that store and give a signal to her friend Kara who would be working there tonight. Kara would have a fake message to give to Lily that would cause Lily to have to leave immediately. But her escape plan wasn’t needed. So the back-up plan wouldn’t be needed either. She felt it important to go to that store and tell Kara that all was well. So she led Zeke down the Boscov's mall towards Bath & Body Works.

"I have a dream nursery," she said as she slowly walked hand-in-hand with him down the mall. "It's a dream nursery in my mind."

"Oh yeah? What does it look like?" he asked.

"The walls are pink with colorful butterfly stickers all over the place. There is a crib with pink Disney Princess sheets, and it's loaded so full with teddy bears that there is just enough for me to lay down in it," she said as her eyes envision it in her mind. In the far corner of the room, there is a toy chest filled with every toy that I used to play with as little girl."

"What toys are in it?" he asked.

"My Little Pony, Rainbow Brite, Cabbage Patch Dolls, and Barbies, galore of course," she said with a giggle and a smile.

"Of course," he said, smiling.

"Oh! And also She-ra the Princess of Power," she quickly added. "I bet you don't know who she is."

"She-Ra is the sister which He-man never knew he had," he replied.

She looked at him with a delighted surprise.

“I’m impressed,” she said. “Do you remember how they finally met?”

“No, but I remember he met her in the cartoon movie that was released to the theaters,” he answered trying to recall.

“How did they meet?”

“I don’t remember either,” she admitted, laughing. “I was hoping you knew.”

She paused for a moment, looking over at him. There had to be something wrong with him. He couldn’t possibly be this good. Up to this point, he hadn’t over-stepped her boundaries once. He had no idea where she lived, and he didn’t pressure her to tell him.

She lowered her eyes for a moment as she got shy and brought them back up to gaze at him.

“There’s a changing table in the corner by the closet,” she said with bashfulness. “It has everything needed to … change me. Complete with four different kinds of diapers.”

“Really?” he asked, with a smile. “What else is in this dream room?”

"A bookshelf with every Little Golden Book ever published along with a complete collection of Dr. Seuss books, coloring books, and bed time story books," she said, lightly nibbling on her bottom lip as she awaited his reaction.

"Is there a rocking chair next to the crib so you can be cradled while these bed time stories are read to you?" he asked.

"You betcha," she said as she did her best to contain her excitement.

"And do you have a special place where you sit when coloring in your coloring books?" he asked.

"Uh-huh," she said as her smile grew. "It's in the middle of the room. I lay on my tummy on a rainbow-colored rug," she said. "And I have a big bucket of crayons. There are also night lights in every outlet to keep the room from getting too dark at night, and to keep my fingers out of the sockets."

"That sounds like a very smart idea," he said. "Do you sleep in the crib at night?"

"I always take my afternoon naps in my crib," she answered. "But at night, I sleep where my Daddy lays me down. "Hopefully, I'm in Daddy's bed with him some of the time. But a BabyGirl should sleep in a crib some of the time as well."

They both shared a set of smiles as they entered the Bath & Body Works store. Kara, Lily's friend who worked there, dropped what she was doing and practically bolted over to them.

"Lily!" Kara said in a panicked tone. "I'm so glad you stopped in. I just got a call from…"

"Kara…" Lily said, quickly cutting her off. "This is Zeke. Zeke, this is Kara."

"Hello," Kara said with a concerned look as she shook his hand. "Did you guys have a … nice …… dinner?"

She was still uncertain as to whether Lily had approved of him.

"Yes, we ate at Damon's," she said calmly as she touched Kara's arm, trying to signal everything was okay. "It was wonderful. By chance did you guys get any of the butterfly flower scent in the lotions you were out of the other day?"

Kara's face brightened up as a smile formed from ear to ear.

"Not yet, but we ordered them," Kara said with a look of playful interest. "So, umm, what did you guys talk about at dinner, Zeke?"

There was a moment of awkward silence. Zeke looked at Lily who had opened her eyes wide and stared at him intently, trying to send him a message. He looked back at Kara who was grinning without reserve.

"We talked about everything we could think of," he answered safely.

"Such as….?" she asked, not allowing him to get away from answering so easily.

Zeke paused for another moment, and then courageously replied.

"We spoke of our fondest memories and of the things we shared in common," he said. "We spoke of what was in our hearts, what made us happy and what dreams may come."

"We need to get going, Kara," Lily said quickly before Kara could prod any further. "Let me know when that lotion comes in."

"I certainly will," Kara said, watching them leave the store." Butterfly flower. Nice meeting you, Zeke."

"That was really scary," Lily said as they headed towards the center court of the mall. "She doesn't know about my little side, but has always suspected something was up."

"The danger of discovery," Zeke remarked.

"I was getting the tummy butterflies as she did her cross-examination of you," she said.

"You have this obsession with butterflies," he said.

"Obsession?" she asked. "What do you mean?"

"Butterflies in your tummy when you get nervous or when you get excited or when you almost get discovered," he explained. "And butterfly flower shampoo."

"No," she corrected. "It's a skin lotion."

"Whatever it is. The point is this…." Zeke said. "…a butterfly represents many things. One of which is long life."

"What else does a butterfly represent?" she asked, intrigued.

"Butterflies also represent rebirth. From a caterpillar to a cocoon, reborn into a butterfly," he answered. "The name Lily also means rebirth."

"So I'm supposed to wrap myself into a cocoon and be reborn as a butterfly," she said with a laugh.

"Not exactly," he said, sharing her humor. "But you definitely have some sort of connection with the butterfly."

"It's amazing that a butterfly represents long life and I get butterflies in my tummy, even though I deal with stomach pains from time to time that hurt so bad I want to die."

"Really?" he asked, concerned. "You ought to see a doctor about that."

"It's nothing, just a little indigestion," she said, blowing the subject off as to not draw any attention to it. "My name also means purity and sometimes fertility. What does the name Zeke mean?"

"It means God will Strengthen," he said. "I'm not sure how that relates to me."

So the butterflies in my tummy and my name mean that I am pure, fertile and destined to be reborn. And you will be made stronger by God," she summarized.

"It's interesting that we both have found a love for ABDL," he said. "I'm a Daddy and you are a Nena."

"A what?" she asked.

"It's Spanish for BabyGirl," he responded.

"Really?" she said, laughing. "What is it in German?"

"Töchterchen,"

"Holland?"

"Meisje."

"How do you know these words?" she asked. "Do you speak all these languages?"

"Nope," he answered. "But last night I memorized how to say BabyGirl in all those languages so I could impress you today."

Lily paused for a moment, staring at him with a smile on her face. Then she broke out into laughter.

"Okay. Impress me some more," she said, enjoying this. "How about in Italian?"

"Neonata," he answered quickly.

"Swedish?"

"Barnflicka."

"Portugal?"

"Menina de Bebê."

"Turkey?"

"Bebek Kız."

"Romania?"

"Fetito."

"I like that one … Fetito," she said, sounding it out slowly. "What about French?"

"Petitee Fille," he answered while seeing something that interested him in the clothing store they were passing by. "Or… bébé."

Zeke took her by the hand, led her into the store and straight to a rack of clothing. Lily looked at the t-shirt hanging in front of her. It was a pink, short-sleeved shirt that had the word "Bebe" on the front with butterflies underneath it.

"It is amazing, isn't it," he said, taking the shirt to the register and buying it for her.

Lily was really enjoying herself. Zeke was very easy to get along with and he made her laugh and laugh often with his silliness. At the same time, his charm had found a way to touch her heart. Being by his side felt so right and so good. Could she have actually found who she was looking for?

They ventured out of the store and Lily looked up at the store sign one more time.

"Bebe," she said, smiling widely.

They made their way back to the center of the mall and started heading towards the J.C. Penney's wing. Lily looked across the center court over to the Bon Ton wing.

"Do you sniff candles?" she asked abruptly.

"Do I what?" he asked back, perplexed.

"Whenever I come to Park City Mall I always go to the Yankee Candle Store and sniff the candles," she replied.

"Really?" he asked. "Well, then I think we should go do that.

They made their way to the Yankee Candle store and as they entered the scent of candles filled the air. Lily went straight over to the walls and started open the jars and smelling the candles.

"What scent of candle do you normally buy?" he asked.

"Oh, I never buy them. I just like to smell them. Here, smell this," she said as she handed him a jar.

"Woah … Cinnamon," he said, pulling his nose back from the jar.

"Apple Cinnamon, actually," she said, taking the jar from him and putting it back on the shelf.

She went from wall to wall and from table to table sniffing all the candles.

"I wonder how many people have sniffed these candles inside a day's time," he said.

"Probably a lot," she said, handing him another jar. "Smell this one."

"Okay," he said, smelling it. "What's it called?"

"Sun and Sand," she replied. "Smell this one."

"What's this one called?" he asked, sniffing it.

"Ocean Water," she said.

"They both remind me of the beach," he said.

"I've never been to the beach," she said, smelling them both again before setting them back down.

"Never?" he asked, surprised.

"Never," she replied.

"Would you like to some day?" he asked as they started to leave the store.

"Oh yes," she said, enthusiastically.

“Well then. That settles it,” he said. “I’m going to take you to the beach.”

“Really?” she asked playfully as they left the store and headed back to the food court. “What beach?”

“What beach do you want to go to?” he asked. “Take your pick. We’ll go there.”

“Okay,” she said, playing along. “How about … the Bahamas?”

“Done,” he said.

“You are going to take me to the Bahamas?” she said smiling, yet not believing him at all. “I don’t believe you.”

“Not only will I take you to the Bahamas,” he said. “But the entire time, you will be my fetito … my BabyGirl.”

“You mean I will be your baby on this beach trip?” she asked, giggling.

“Every second of it,” he answered.

“I still don’t believe you,” she said.

“If I were to make that happen…a vacation to the Bahamas…would you go?” he asked as he looked at another store they were passing by in the J.C. Penney's wing. "Certainly after we got to know one another better, and if things grew between us. Would you go?"

Lily looked at him with disbelief.

"Yeah," she said for certain. "If you were to set that up, I definitely go, and I would definitely be your baby for the whole trip."

Zeke led her into the store they were passing by.

"Then we'll need to get you a stuffed animal for the trip," he said as she saw the store he took her into.

"Build-a-Bear!" she said, jumping up and down and clapping her hands quickly.

"Why don't you make one?" he asked as he encouraged her.

She went up to the bins and looked at the different types of stuffed animals. There were Horses, unicorns, puppies, floppy-earred bunnies, frogs, moose, leopards, polar bears, camouflaged bears, monkeys, Hello Kitty, gray wolves, and even Darth Vader.

Lily chose a simple brown teddy bear. She carried it over to the stuffer lady at the stuffing machine and handed it to her.

"Well, hello there," the stuffer lady said with a smile, seeing the twinkle in Lily's eyes and her indulgent demeanor.

The lady was a bit older and put some enjoyment into her work, giving it the maximum "make-believe" possible. Adults going through the build-a-bear line were nothing out of the ordinary. She attached the bear to the stuffer machine and began filling it with fluff.

"Have you named your teddy bear yet?" the lady asked with a grin.

"Yep," Lily said, enthusiastically. "Teddy."

"I think this bear is going to be well loved by you," the lady said as she finished stuffing the bear. "Do you think you ought to put two hearts inside it?"

Lily smiled and nodded slightly.

"Well, pick two out of the bin and rub them together so they the bear will have a two warm hearts to love you with," the lady said.

Lily rubbed them together as instructed.

"Now press them against your heart so the bear's heart will beat in rhythm with yours," the lady said.

Lily pressed the hearts against her chest and handed them to the lady. She put them inside the bear and sewed his back shut with string.

“And now the most important thing,” the lady said, handing the bear to Lily. “The first hug … make it a good one so he knows you love him.”

Lily hugged the bear as she turned to Zeke with a smile. Zeke winked at her.

“Do you want any clothes for it?” Zeke asked while leading her over to the bear clothes section.

“No,” she said, hugging the bear tightly for dear life. “He’s perfect as he is.”

Lily went through the certificate process at the computer and got the bear box when they went to the counter. They exited the store, hand in hand, and strolled down the rest of the J.C. Penney’s wing. They didn’t say much to each other, just simply sharing smiles as they stepped onto the escalator, heading down to the food court.

Zeke stopped at the last food stand before the exit.

“This is a tradition of mine when I come here,” he said. “A cinnamon pretzel from Auntie Anne’s for the road.”

“It sounds like a tasty pretzel,” she said.

“Two cinnamon pretzels please,” Zeke said to the lady behind the counter.

They strolled out the door and into the parking lot, in no particular hurry. They walked to her car and sat on the trunk, looking up at the stars as they finished the pretzels.

“Zik, Wull Yih go entu wahn mow stoh wit mee?” she asked with a mouthful of soft pretzel.

“I think that was a question, but I’m not sure,” he said as she laughed and then swallowed her food.

“Will you go into one more store with me?” she asked. “I still have one more thing to pick up. I always get one of these as well when I come here.”

“Absolutely. What store?” he asked.

“It’s over in the plaza stores across the road,” she said. “Follow me.”

She jumped into her car and Zeke walked over to his car. He followed her out of the J.C. Penney’s / Sears parking lot and turned left on Plaza Drive. A smile came to his face when he saw the store parking lot she turned into.

“Babies-R-Us. You little angel, you,” he thought as he parked next to her.

She got out of the car and looked over at him with a playful grin.

"What do you need from here?" he asked as they walked in.

Lily went straight to the second aisle on the left and selected a pacifier.

"I always buy one of these when I come to Park City Mall," she said.

"And how many of them do you have?" he asked as they made their way to the register.

"About 30, I think," she said paying the cashier and walking out of the store with him.

"I can't imagine you use all of them," he said as they crossed the parking lot.

"Oh my goodness, No," she said. "I have three that I use. I don't even open the others. I just collect them."

"Okay. You have an obsession with butterflies you weren't even aware of. You buy pacifiers and don't use them," he said as she laughed and then embraced him.

"And now I have a Daddy," she said as he returned the embrace.

"And now I have a Fetito," he said as he stroked the hair on the back of her head.

"When can we do this again?" she asked.

"Soon," he replied. "You're going to need a new bathing suit."

"And a diaper bag," she said playfully. "Good bye, Ezekiel Williams."

"Good bye, Lily Paddington," he said.

"I'll be in touch … very soon," she said as she got into her car and drove home.

Zeke watched her car driving away until it disappeared beyond the overpass on Harrisburg Pike, headed back into Lancaster City. He made his way to his car. No sooner did he sit down and start the car then his cell phone buzzed with a message from Lily.

He opened the message and it read:

"I told you it would be soon. I should have asked you to change me before I left. lol Next time for sure.

TTYS, Fetito."

The End

Zorro Daddy's Complete ABDL Library

Gabriel and Gina

When Gina revealed a love for a fetish to a friend during a drunken Saturday night college party, she had no idea that she would be living out that fetish with him in a few short days.

On this autumn weekend at a college campus, Gina sees her most erotic wishes come true as she learns how much she enjoys being submissive. Her fantasies become a reality, heating up at the end in a sexual climax that leaves her body and her mind in a state of absolute ecstasy.

This story is a romantic fantasy with heavy sexual content, situations and actions. It is adult material and not intended for anyone under the age of 18.

Rock-a-Bye BabyGirls: *Thoughts and Other Journeys of the Mind*

These are short writings that touch upon the emotions felt by the male and female in an infantilism role playing setting and/or relationship. Topics include, but are not limited to: concepts of feeling little, the attachments to and emotional affects of having and using baby items, security, safety, comfort, helplessness, vulnerability, love, respect, overcoming fears and alibis, exploring one's deepest desire, and one's most well kept secrets.

Every writing builds off the previous one in concept and appeal. Nothing in this section is written in story format. Names and locations are generalized and not defined.

Rock-a-Bye BabyGirls: *Short and Sweet Stories*

These are writings which are written in a loose story format. Some are in a style of a love letter that he wrote to her, thoughts within his mind as he watches her role play, his reflections and remembrances of previous role playing encounters with her, recalled thoughts of her which further strengthens his adoration and love for her, and lists desires, wishes, wants, needs, cravings and pride within his heart and soul.

Names and locations are generalized and not defined.

The Zeke and Lily Stories

Before Zeke (an author) and Lily (a newspaper columnist) met, they were perfect strangers who shared a common interest in a role playing fetish. They were perfect for each other and though they lived in the same city, they may never have met until Lily happened upon Zeke's profile online.

This collection of stories tells their tale, from courting to love to a possible happily ever after.

Zeke and Lily: *Once Upon a Beginning*

The story of the day they first met face-to-face at a mall in Lancaster County, PA.

Zeke and Lily: *Overnight*

Zeke and Lily spend the night in his apartment. The result is an evening of events where their separate lives finally collide and they fall in love. By morning, their fantasies had turned into their reality together. But will it lead to a "happily ever after" for them?

Zeke and Lily: *Making a Memory*

Zeke and Lily have bonded their hearts. Their common interest in infantilism has grown into a love for each other. As they head off on a Bahamas vacation, that love deepens. But trouble is on the horizon.

Lily, still letting go of her troubled past, has a secret she deliberately kept from Zeke. Her fear that he will no longer love her increases and she begins to get sick over the decision to tell him the truth.

Zeke has a question to ask Lily. It is a question that is weighing on his heart.

As they enjoy their time in the Caribbean, they both struggle within to overcome their fears. But something happens while in the Bahamas that delays their chance to get the truth out, and they may not recover.

Do Zeke and Lily come home together or did their fantasy love just die in the Bahamas?

www.ingramcontent.com/pod-product-compliance
Ingram Content Group UK Ltd.
Pitfield, Milton Keynes, MK11 3LW, UK
UKHW020230250726
13967UKWH00001B/277

9 780557 342693